THE CHRISTMAS DONKEY

For Pat and David

THE CHRISTMAS DONKEY

Gillian McClure

A Sunburst Book
Farrar Straus Giroux

There was once a donkey dealer who had three donkeys. Two of them, Ebed and Obed, were gentle, obedient creatures. The third, Arod, made trouble whenever he could. "Too wild and proud," the donkey dealer would often mutter.

One day, when the donkey dealer was in the stable grooming Ebed and Obed, news came that all the people in the land had to return to the town of their birth to pay their taxes.

"And how will they travel?" the dealer asked himself happily. "By donkey, of course. Everyone will need a donkey. With the money I'll get for these three, I can buy six more. There'll be no end to it."

At that moment, Arod came into the stable, upset the water bucket with his head, and kicked it against the wall. "And you'll be the first to go," the man shouted at him.

The first traveler to arrive was a rich baker, and the dealer wasted no time in showing him Arod. "You won't regret it if you take this one," he said. "He's keen-eyed and sure-footed."

But the baker saw the wildness in Arod's eyes and thought differently. "No, not that one," he said. "But I'll pay you in gold for this one," he added, pointing to Ebed. So the deal was done. As the baker left, Arod stole a loaf from his bag. "A richer man than you will choose me," he brayed angrily. "Only a king is good enough for me."

The next to arrive was a wealthy wine merchant. Again the dealer pointed to Arod. "This is the animal for you," he said. "Keen-eyed and sure-footed." Arod kicked out his hind leg. "No, not that one," said the merchant firmly. "But I'll pay you in silver for this one." And he took hold of Obed's bridle.

Arod tore the wine merchant's robe with his strong teeth. "Just wait," he snorted. "My king will come, a finer man than you'll ever be."

A little later, a poor carpenter arrived. His wife, Mary, was going to have a baby soon and he needed a donkey to carry her to Bethlehem. "You're lucky," said the dealer. "I have one donkey left and he is my best: keen-eyed and sure-footed, gentle and brave."

Joseph hesitated. "I don't have much money ..." he began. "He's yours," said the donkey dealer hurriedly. But Arod had other ideas. This man was no king. Arod wanted to run, but there in the doorway stood Mary. Arod bowed his head and let her climb on his back.

The donkey dealer watched them go. "The others will arrive safely," he thought, "but I am afraid Arod will give those two nothing but trouble."

For a while Arod trudged along the stony road; then his patience began to run out. He spotted a patch of thistles and lunged toward them, hoping to shake off his heavy burden. Suddenly he heard a strange roaring in his ears and stopped short.

Joseph came running up. "You are indeed brave," he said. "I didn't see that lion blocking the path. You have saved our lives."

Mary stroked Arod's neck gently, and as they set off once more, his load seemed lighter.

On and on they traveled. Arod grew tired, and as night fell, he spotted some wild goats grazing in a meadow and decided to join them. But a falling star flashed across the sky, startling him, and he reared up sharply.

"Oh, donkey," said Joseph. "I failed to see the snake curled in the shadows. But, thanks to your sharp eyes, we can go safely on our way."

Arod was pleased, and as Mary patted him lovingly, the stars shone brighter.

The next day, their route took them down into deep
valleys. Arod hated it. He jerked his head away from
Joseph and was about to bolt when a shining figure
appeared before him. Joseph caught Arod's reins.

"You are as sure-footed as we were told," he said gratefully.
"We would certainly have fallen into that ravine."

Mary caressed the donkey's velvety ears. Arod walked on.
The path was less stony and his burden much lighter now.

At last Joseph, Mary, and Arod reached a hill above
Bethlehem. As they watched a stream of travelers
passing through the gates, Joseph said sadly to Mary,
"It will be hard to find a room for you to rest in
tonight."

But Arod was untroubled. He trotted calmly on,
carrying Mary proudly through the gates.

At the first inn they visited, the innkeeper just laughed.
"You're far too late," he said, guffawing. "The whole
world got here before you."

Arod, meanwhile, had gone to the stable at the back of the inn. There he met Ebed, smugly chewing a mouthful of hay. "You'll never find a room in Bethlehem," Ebed said. "You must have dawdled. I brought my rich baker straight here and he's comfortably settled."

Arod snorted. "I carried something more precious than any baker," he said.

At the second inn, Joseph fared no better. "Be off with you," shouted the innkeeper. "Can't you see we're full?"

At the back of this inn Arod found Obed, looking pleased with himself. "You must have lost your way," Obed said. "The town's full up, you know. My wine merchant was very content with the smooth, swift ride I gave him."

"My charge was worth a hundred wine merchants and all their wine," retorted Arod.

At the third inn, the innkeeper's wife took pity on Mary. "You won't find a room anywhere," she said. "But we can give you stable space, if you like. It's warm and dry."

So Arod led Mary and Joseph to the stable. He told the ox, the sheep, and the hens to make room for Mary, who lay down on the straw. A strange light filled the darkness, and the air was still.

Then they heard a cry – the cry of a newborn baby. The animals moved closer and knelt before Mary, Joseph, and the baby.

"Lay him in my manger," lowed the ox.

"Cover him with our hay," bleated the sheep.

"Our feathers will make a soft pillow," clucked the hens.

There was no room for Arod to kneel with the others, so he nipped the ox on the rump. The ox jumped, the sheep baaed, the hens flew up to the rafters, and Arod knelt down before his king. "Thank you for choosing me," he brayed softly.

The baby smiled.